PUFFIN BOOKS

THE WITCH'S DOG
AND THE TREASURE MAP

Frank Rodgers has written and illustrated a wide range of books for children: picture books, story books, non-fiction and novels. His children's stories have been broadcast on radio and TV and a sitcom series based on his book *The Intergalactic Kitchen* was created for CBBC. His recent work for Puffin includes the bestselling Witch's Dog and Robodog titles and the swashbuckling Pirate Penguins series. Frank was an art teacher before becoming an author and illustrator and he lives in Glasgow with his wife. He has two grown-up children.

D0543702

Books by Frank Rodgers for younger readers

THE WITCH'S DOG

THE WITCH'S DOG AT THE
SCHOOL OF SPELLS

THE WITCH'S DOG AND THE
MAGIC CAKE

THE WITCH'S DOG AND THE
CRYSTAL BALL

THE WITCH'S DOG AND THE
FLYING CARPET

THE WITCH'S DOG AND THE
ICE-CREAM WIZARD

THE WITCH'S DOG AND THE
BOX OF TRICKS

THE WITCH'S DOG AND THE
TALKING PICTURE

THE WITCH'S DOG AND THE
TREASURE MAP

PIRATE PENGUINS

PIRATE PENGUINS AND THE
SARDINES OF DOOM

THE ROBODOG

THE ROBODOG AND THE BIG DIG

THE BUNK-BED BUS

Frank Rodgers

The Witch's Dog and the Treasure Map

PUFFIN

PUFFIN BOOKS

Published by the Penguin Group
Penguin Books Ltd, 80 Strand, London WC2R 0RL, England
Penguin Group (USA) Inc., 375 Hudson Street, New York, New York 10014, USA
Penguin Group (Canada), 90 Eglinton Avenue East, Suite 700, Toronto, Ontario, Canada M4P 2Y3
(a division of Pearson Penguin Canada Inc.)
Penguin Ireland, 25 St Stephen's Green, Dublin 2, Ireland (a division of Penguin Books Ltd)
Penguin Group (Australia), 250 Camberwell Road, Camberwell, Victoria 3124, Australia
(a division of Pearson Australia Group Pty Ltd)
Penguin Books India Pvt Ltd, 11 Community Centre, Panchsheel Park, New Delhi – 110 017, India
Penguin Group (NZ), 67 Apollo Drive, Rosedale, North Shore 0632, New Zealand
(a division of Pearson New Zealand Ltd)
Penguin Books (South Africa) (Pty) Ltd, 24 Sturdee Avenue,
Rosebank, Johannesburg 2196, South Africa

Penguin Books Ltd, Registered Offices: 80 Strand, London WC2R 0RL, England

puffinbooks.com

First published 2008
2

Text and illustrations copyright © Frank Rodgers, 2008
All rights reserved

The moral right of the author/illustrator has been asserted

Set in Times New Roman Schoolbook
Made and printed in Singapore by Star Standard

British Library Cataloguing in Publication Data
A CIP catalogue record for this book is available from the British Library

ISBN: 978-0-141-32185-1

Wilf, the witch's dog, was singing at the top of his voice. "I'm the jolly cook for a pirate crew. I love to cook up jolly tasty pirate stews. Yo, ho, ho!"

Wilf was rehearsing for the school show, which was taking place that day in the park. It was a musical about pirates, and Wilf had the part of the pirate cook.

YO HO HO!

A pirate musical in the park.

He was going to wear a bright blue jacket and red sash.

Weenie, the witch, had washed them
that morning and hung them in the
garden. They were dry now and Wilf
was eager to try them on.

As he went
through to the
kitchen he saw
that Weenie was
busy searching
in a drawer.

"What are you looking for, Weenie?"
asked Wilf.

Weenie sighed. "I've lost a letter from
my cousin Charlie," she said. "He's
the Head Chef at the Wizard School
of Cookery. We're going to make a
delicious picnic for your after-show
party.

"He sent me a list of ingredients to buy but I can't remember where I put it."

"I'll help you look for it as soon as I've fetched my pirate costume from the washing line," said Wilf.

"Back in a tick."

Outside, Sly Cat and Tricky Toad were looking over Weenie's garden gate. They were witches' pets too, and they were jealous of Wilf because he was going to be the star of the school show.

Sly glanced at Wilf's pirate costume flapping in the breeze and winked at Tricky.

"It's a very windy day, isn't it, Tricky?" he said. "What a pity it would be if Wilf's costume blew away."

Tricky sniggered. "What a pity," he repeated.

Quickly, they sent out a super-strong wind spell.

It shot across the garden, whirled round Wilf's costume, and . . .

WHOOSH

. . . blew it high
into the air.
As the jacket soared over
Sly and Tricky's heads, a
piece of paper fell from
a pocket and fluttered to
the ground.

Sly picked it up.

"Looks like this has been through
the wash," he muttered. "The
writing's all smudged. I can't read
what it says." He turned it over.
"But look at this . . .
there's a map
on the back."

"It fell out of a pirate jacket," said
Tricky excitedly, "so it could be a
treasure map!"
"You could be right," answered Sly.

Just then Wilf came into the garden.
"My costume!" he gasped as he

spotted his jacket
and sash heading
for the clouds.

"How did that happen?"

"It's a very windy
day, Wilf," said
Sly innocently,
hiding the map
behind his back.

"Very windy,"
echoed Tricky.

Sniggering together, they
hurried away.

Wilf frowned. He
suspected that Sly
and Tricky had
something to do
with it and
wondered what
they were up to.

Quickly fetching his broomstick, he
leapt aboard and . . .

ZOOM

. . . shot off after
his escaping pirate
costume.

Flying at top speed, he soon caught
up with the jacket and sash . . .

but getting hold of them was a
different matter.
The sash snapped and twisted in the
wind . . .

and the jacket flipped and flopped
this way and that.

Wilf looped
the loop . . .

did power dives . . .

and even had to fly upside down as
he chased them all over the sky.

At last, zooming round in a tight turn, he managed to snatch his costume from the air.

Tucking the jacket and sash safely under his arm, Wilf flew back down to the garden just as his friends were arriving.

Harry, Bertie and Streaky were all in pirate costume. They were going to be in the musical too.

"I still can't find Charlie's letter," said Weenie as Wilf and his friends came into the kitchen.

"He'll be here at any moment and Charlie will think I have already bought the ingredients for the picnic.

"But I don't know what to buy."

"Perhaps you can use what you've got in the food cupboard, Weenie," suggested Wilf.

"Good idea!" cried Weenie and she rushed to the cupboard.

But her face fell when she looked inside.

"All I have is some flour, a few apples, a bit of butter, and sugar and salt," she groaned. "What kind of picnic can I make from that?"

"Have no fear . . . Charlie's here!" called a voice from the door.

Everyone turned to see Charlie, the wizard chef, standing in the doorway. He was holding a big bag of shopping.

"The shopkeeper told me you hadn't bought anything yet, Weenie," said Charlie. "So I got all the ingredients."

Weenie smiled in delight. "Thank you, Charlie," she said. "Let's get started on making that picnic!"

As Weenie and Charlie set to work, Wilf and his friends said goodbye and left for the park.

"See you later, Weenie," called Wilf.

At the park, Sly and Tricky were
lurking behind the stage.
Tricky was holding up the map.
"I'm sure this is a treasure map,
Sly," he said.

"Hold it still while I put a spell on it, Tricky," Sly said.

"Let's see if it brings us any treasure."

"Oh yes . . . treasure," echoed Tricky greedily.

Sly aimed a spell at the map and . . .

FLASH!

. . . the map glowed with a bright
light. But the light faded quickly and
nothing seemed to happen.
Then Sly looked up.

"What's that thing in the sky?" he
asked.

"I don't know – but it's coming towards us very fast," said Tricky.

Sly stared in amazement. "It . . . it . . . it's a pirate ship!" he yelped. "My spell's gone wrong!"

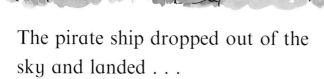

The pirate ship dropped out of the sky and landed . . .

CRASH!

. . . right on top of the stage.

Sly and Tricky
tried to run . . .

but were caught
in a net thrown
from the ship.

They were hauled
up and left
dangling like a
catch of fish.

The pirate captain stormed across
the deck.

"One minute we're sailing along
quite happily," he shouted, "and the
next . . . *flash!* . . . we're stuck in the
middle of a blooming park!"

He pointed at Sly and Tricky.

"And I'm sure you're to blame for this," he growled.

Sly and Tricky swallowed nervously.

Just then, Wilf and his friends came into the park.
Wilf had put on his costume and was singing at the top of his voice again.

"I'm the jolly cook for a pirate crew. I love to cook up jolly tasty pirate stews. Yo, ho, ho!"

"Enemy pirates on the starboard bow!" cried the pirate captain. He turned to his crew.

"Quick . . . let's capture them!"

Swiftly, he and his crew leapt from the ship.

Suddenly Wilf, Harry, Bertie and Streaky found themselves trapped by fearsome pirates.

"So, matey," said the captain, staring closely at Wilf, "you're a cook, eh? Excellent!

"Just what we've been looking for. Our own cook ran away to be a hairdresser last week and we haven't had a decent meal since.

"The crew and I have tried to cook for ourselves but we're just no good at it."

"But – " began Wilf.

"No buts!" roared the captain.

"Cook us up a tasty meal right now. If you don't, we'll make you all walk the plank.

"Once we get back to the sea, that is," he added quickly.

Wilf was about to protest again when
he saw Weenie and Charlie arriving.
Between them they carried a large
hamper full of the food they had
made for the after-show picnic. A
delicious smell was wafting from it.

Wilf shouted
a warning:
"Weenie . . .
Charlie . . . run!
These are
real pirates!"

But the pirates were too quick for
them. A moment later, Weenie and
Charlie had been captured too.

"What's going on, Wilf?" Weenie
said in confusion, looking around.
"Are these *really* real pirates?"

"Oh yes, indeed we are," replied the
captain with a nasty grin. "So we'll
take that lovely food you've
brought, thank you very much."

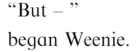
"But – "
began Weenie.

"No buts!" roared
the captain and
he opened the
hamper.

He and the crew looked inside.
"Mmmm," they said, licking their
lips. "Lovely grub!"

They all began to gobble the food greedily.

There was nothing that Weenie, Charlie, Wilf or his friends could do.

In a few minutes there wasn't a crumb left. The pirates sighed contentedly.

"That was the best meal I've ever had," said the captain.
"The best," agreed the crew.

"I wish I could cook like that," the captain went on.
"Me too," said each of the crew.

"And I wish I was a pirate," said Charlie all of a sudden.

Everyone looked at him in surprise.

"You do?" asked Weenie.

"Oh yes," replied Charlie. "I've wanted to be a pirate ever since I was a little chef. I still like to dress up as a pirate and draw pirate maps for fun.

"In fact," he went on, "I drew a treasure map on the back of your letter, Weenie."

Above them they heard a gasp of
surprise. Looking up, they saw Sly
and Tricky dangling in the net.
Charlie pointed to
the piece of paper
that Sly still
clutched in his
hand.

"That's it!" he cried. "My treasure
map. Where did you get it?"

Sly and Tricky looked down miserably.

"It was in Wilf's pirate jacket," said Sly.

"So that's where I put it!" exclaimed Weenie. "I am silly."

"We thought the map was real," said Tricky.

Weenie looked stern. "So," she said, "you used a spell on it to get the treasure . . . and instead you got pirates."

"You certainly did," retorted the
captain. "And we got you! You're
all going to walk the plank. Er . . .
once we get back to the sea, that is,"
he added again quickly.

Suddenly Wilf had an idea.

"Did you really mean it when you said you'd like to be good cooks?" he asked the captain.

"Of course," the captain replied, and his crew nodded in agreement. "Of course."

"Well," said Wilf, "this is Charlie. He is the Head Chef at the Wizard School of Cookery. I'm sure he could teach you how to be brilliant cooks."

47

The captain and his crew turned to
Charlie excitedly.
"Could you?" they asked.

Charlie beamed with delight.
"Of course I could!" he cried.

"It would tickle
me pink to
teach you."

"Then what are we waiting for?"
boomed the captain.

"Let's go to the Wizard School of
Cookery right now."
"Wonderful," said Charlie. "Let's go!"

Before they left,
the captain
presented Charlie
with his best
skull-and-
crossbones
pirate hat.

Charlie was thrilled. "I feel like a
real pirate at last!" he cried.
"Yo, ho, ho!"

Then he said goodbye to everyone
and with a cheerful wave he strode
off with the happy pirates.

Wilf remembered something.

"But, captain," he called after them,
"what about your ship?"
"Keep it!" cried the captain over his
shoulder. "We're going to be chefs
so we won't be needing it again.
You can use it as a replacement for
your broken stage."

So that's what they did.

That evening, Wilf and his friends performed in the pirate musical *Yo, Ho, Ho!* It was a great success.

Everybody was thrilled that the show had taken place on a real pirate ship.

Even Sly and Tricky enjoyed it. Wilf
had given them front-row seats
because, for once, their mischief had
accidentally caused something nice to
happen.

But as the cast met after the show,
Weenie groaned in disappointment.

"Oh no," she said. "In all the excitement I forgot to make more things to eat for the after-show picnic. And I only know cookery spells that can be used on real food." That gave Wilf another idea.

"Don't worry, Weenie," he said, grinning. "I know exactly what to do."

He turned to Streaky and whispered
in his ear.

Streaky
grinned too.

"Back in a tick, Wilf," he said and
zoomed off at top speed.

"Where has Streaky
gone?" asked Bertie.

"You'll see," said
Wilf mysteriously.

A moment later, speedy Streaky was back.

And in his paws was a box containing a bag of flour, some apples, a butter dish, and sugar and salt.

"You got those from my kitchen cupboard," said Weenie with a smile. "And I think I know what you're going to do with them, Wilf."

Wilf smiled back. "A little bit of magic that you taught me, Weenie," he replied.

Everyone watched eagerly as Wilf sent out a spell.

It sparkled around the flour, apples, butter, sugar and salt for a second and then . . .

FLASH!

. . . the ingredients were transformed into an extra-delicious, giant-size, home-made apple pie. It smelt wonderful.

"You're a genius, Wilf!" cried Weenie, and everyone cheered.

Soon, the after-show picnic was in full swing – everybody was enjoying Wilf's tasty apple pie.

"You turned out to be a pirate cook after all, Wilf," said Harry, munching happily.

Wilf laughed and took a big slice of pie. "Yo, ho, ho!" he cried. "Or should I say . . .

. . . yum, yum, yum!"